LEARNING TO BE CAPTAIN

LEARNING TO BE CAPTAIN

By
SCOTT YOUNG

Illustrations by
KENNETH M. SHIELDS

EMC Corporation
St. Paul, Minnesota

Library of Congress Cataloging in Publication Data

Young, Scott.
   Learning to be captain.

   (His Face-off series)
   SUMMARY: As captain of his school hockey team, Billy faces a morale problem when a new boy becomes famous by doing all the scoring.
   [1. Hockey—Stories]   I. Shields, Kenneth M., illus. II. Title.
PZ7.Y879Le   [Fic]   73-4354
ISBN 0-912022-58-2
ISBN 0-912022-53-1 (pbk)

Text© 1973 by Ascot Productions, Limited
Illustrations© 1973 by EMC Corporation
All rights reserved. Published 1973
Published by EMC Corporation
180 East Sixth Street
St. Paul, Minnesota 55101
Published simultaneously in Canada by
J.M. Dent & Sons (Canada) Limited,
Don Mills, Ontario
Printed in the United States of America
0987654321

FACE-OFF SERIES

LEARNING TO BE CAPTAIN

THE SILENT ONE SPEAKS UP

FACE-OFF IN MOSCOW

THE MOSCOW CHALLENGERS

Billy Amherst was sitting at the dinner table tearing his paper napkin into pieces. Darn it anyway, how could things that started out so right go so wrong!

Luckily, Billy's mother didn't see the shredded napkin as she came in with his loaded plate. She was smiling, even gushing a little. That was mothers for you.

"It must have been a great feeling to see your name up there on the bulletin board as captain and first-line center," she said, putting the plate in front of him. "Well, you earned it, Billy, with all those mornings of getting up early to improve your skating and shooting."

"I almost wish I wasn't captain now," Billy blurted out.

He saw how surprised she looked. He took a sideways glance at his Dad, who didn't look surprised at all. A little sorry, maybe, but not surprised.

"You shouldn't let Norm Dennison get to you that way, son," Dad said.

"Norm Dennison? You mean the new boy who scores all the goals?" Mother asked. "Why, what has that possibly got to do with you...?"

Billy, poking at his food, glanced up just in time to see Dad shaking his head warningly at Mother, silently telling her to let it drop. Dad changed the subject, right there, when Billy gladly would have gone on. "Tonight is leaf-raking night, right, Billy? Last time this year for that job."

A little later Billy and his father raked leaves silently in the frosty October air. Some kids were playing street hockey at the corner, but Billy didn't even feel like hurrying so that he could join them.

8

"What kind of a kid is Norm Dennison?" Dad asked.

Billy was silent for a minute, but then his words came out in a rush. "Stuck-up. Never talks to anybody. He just . . . just . . . scores his goals in the practices and gets dressed and goes home, as if nobody existed but the great hockey star, Norm Dennison."

"Are you sure you're not saying that just because all the stories in the paper have been about him instead of about you, like they were last year?" asked his father.

Billy kept raking, stubbornly silent. "It's supposed to be a team," he burst out finally. "I mean, there's all the others, too. How do you think they feel when they hear Dennison this, Dennison that, as if nobody else on the team even counts anymore?"

"You're the captain," Dad said. "You're the one who's supposed to make Northern feel like a team, with everybody needing to be part of it, isn't that right? Including Norm Dennison."

Billy didn't say anything more, but he thought, "Fat chance of a guy who plays as well as he does, ever feeling he needed to be part of a team."

Friday night was hockey night in Maple City. Two games for the price of one. When you had four sets of cheerleaders, four student cheering sections and a lot of parents and just plain hockey fans, the crowd could make a lot of noise. It was the only hockey in Maple City, although many people drove forty miles on Saturday nights to watch pro games in the nearest big city.

In the Northern dressing room the players could hear the excited crowd above them. Yet stocky Mac Rutland was silently tying his skates. Little Ali Marchuk had his head down, shoving his leg guards in place. And Billy Amherst, who was usually the main spark plug, always joking and famous for his kidding, never said a word. He silently rolled tape into a ball on the end of a new stick.

"Not like last year," Coach Casey Gordon thought, watching them. Last year he often had to call two or three times for silence before he could make his pre-game speech. He knew what the trouble was, but he also knew it would be better if the kids worked it out for themselves. Coach Gordon only hoped they would work it out soon.

Norm Dennison was the most famous hockey player for miles around. When the coach had first learned that he was enrolling at Northern, because his father had been transferred here, he had been excited and happy. Now he wasn't so sure. Dennison was just so much better than anybody else. He did things so easily that even Billy Amherst, the best of the others on the Northern team, looked almost clumsy in comparison.

"And look at them now," Gordon thought. Everybody was crowded together on the benches, except near Dennison. Dressed and ready, a kid with a thin and sensitive face, Dennison had a good three feet of open space on either side. There'd been another big story about him in the newspaper today.

"All right," the coach called loudly. "Last year we won five games out of ten. This year we can win ten out of ten. I'm serious. Ten out of ten. Let's start tonight with Jefferson Park. Let's get out there and go to it."

When they filed out, Billy Amherst was near the middle of the line and Coach Gordon was at the end just behind Dennison. Since it was the first game, each player was introduced as he stepped to the ice.

"Billy Amherst," the announcer said.

There was a tremendous cheer from the Northern section and it was echoed almost as loudly from other sections. The other players got their share of cheering, too. Finally Dennison skated onto the ice.

"And now, the league's great new star, Norm Dennison!"

The coach winced. The Northern section cheered, but there were boos from other parts of the rink. Obviously some of the fans had been turned off by all the publicity for Dennison, just as the Northern players had.

The coach saw Dennison's helmet tip forward as he dropped his head. How could you tell a boy that in the big world of sports they booed Bobby Orr, too, and Wilt the Stilt, and Johnny Bench? That was the way a crowd often treated a star, the man they had to fear the most.

Coach Gordon looked around and wished that somebody from the Northern team had gone to Dennison and slapped him on the seat of the pants to show the crowd they were with him. Even one of Billy Amherst's corny gags would have helped. But no one went near him.

Billy heard the boos for Dennison. They startled him, and he didn't feel good about it. The cheers he received seemed a little cheap now. Thinking this way took his mind off the game and that could be fatal—a loss of concentration. When the puck was dropped, he was an instant late getting his stick in motion.

The opposing center got the draw, passed to his wing, and skated in on defense. Billy was a half-stride late in following his check. The pass came back, deflected off Mac Rutland's skate, and landed right on the stick of the Jefferson Park center, who was forging in. Goalie Ozzie Burdett, surprised, didn't move out of his goal fast enough to cut down the angle. A quick flick shot and the red light was on. Goal for Jefferson Park.

That woke Billy up. He was glad the coach didn't immediately change lines, as he often did when one line made a bone-headed mistake. "Get going, Billy," he told himself. And he got going. For the next two minutes he was the Billy Amherst that the crowd knew, playing the way that made him so popular both with the fans and with his teammates.

He got the draw from center at the face-off, raced in, lost it, but stayed in the Jefferson end, doggedly forechecking. He broke up one, two, three attempts they made to get out. He streaked over the ice, going into corners, passing back to the blue line, playing in the fast-moving style that was his game.

But when the whistle blew and the line change came, Northern was still down by one goal. Billy couldn't help but blame himself for putting his team behind in the scoring.

When Billy came to the bench he yelled at the others to get the goal back. Dennison didn't look at him, and scattered boos sounded as Dennison skated out to the face-off in the Jefferson Park end. Billy sat forward, leaning on his stick as the puck was dropped.

From there on it was almost too fast for his eyes to follow. Dennison snared the puck and, in a smooth motion, passed it back perfectly to the blue line, then skated for the front of the goal. Rutland shot. It went through a forest of legs. The Jefferson Park goalie had it covered all the way. Dennison didn't even seem to be watching the shot, but his stick blade flicked down at the last instant and bang, deflected the puck into the goal.

Everybody practiced deflections, but usually missed the puck altogether or didn't know where it was going. Dennison made it look so easy, Billy thought; almost lucky.

Behind the bench there was a bellow from a loud-mouthed Jefferson Park supporter. "Dumb luck, Dennison. You can't be that lucky all the time." Billy saw Dennison glance up at the stands, then drop his head as he had when he'd come onto the ice and heard those first boos.

By the end of the game even the loud-mouth had stopped yelling. Dennison got the next three goals. Another was scored by Ali Marchuk on a rebound when the Jefferson goalie was out of position, after stopping a hard shot by Dennison. Northern won 5-2. When newspaper pictures were taken in the dressing room after the game, Dennison naturally was the player the photographer wanted. The star again.

A few weeks later, on the morning after Northern's fourth consecutive win, Billy and most of the other players were in the school cafeteria. They were eating some particularly gooey jelly doughnuts when Mac Rutland came in.

"Hey, Billy," he said. "Coach wants to see you."

Billy got up immediately. He knew the other kids at nearby tables were looking at him. "Gotta plan your strategy for the next one, eh Billy?" someone called. There was a good feeling about being on a winning team.

But the good feeling changed quickly when he sat down in front of the coach's desk. The coach came right to the point. "Billy," he said, "I'm afraid you're not doing your job as captain."

Billy felt his mouth drop open in surprise. "But we're winning," he stammered. "We've never done this well. If we keep going we could win ten out of ten, like you said."

"I guess you were all in the cafeteria when you got my message," Coach Gordon said. "I saw the bunch of you in there. Just about everybody, right?"

"Well, most of them, except Mac, and he's there now."

"And Norm Dennison?" Coach asked.

"Well, no, he isn't there."

"Where's he?" the coach said with an edge in his voice. "Busy studying? Working out in the gym? Or did he go home for lunch today?"

"I don't know."

"You don't know," the coach said. "He's just the guy who's given us four straight wins. We've scored 17 goals and he's got 10 of them. Anybody else scores, you guys pile all over him.

"Norm scores, he's lucky if one guy pats him on the back. Sometimes not even that. Without his goals, we would have won exactly one game. Have you stopped to think of that? One game." Coach Gordon's voice was not raised, but there was no mistaking his mood. "And you and the rest of the guys on the team don't know where he is, or care."

"But Norm just doesn't hang around with the rest of us," Billy protested. "Is that our fault?"

"I think you should ask yourself that question," the coach said. "As captain, ask yourself why it is that one member of your team, whether he happens to be the highest scorer or the lowest scorer, is never with the others except at a practice or a game. How would you feel if it were you being shut out? How would the others feel if it were them. And how do you think Dennison feels?"

Coach Gordon's words had been almost harsh. But then he softened his voice a little and said, "Think about it. That's all, Billy."

Billy thought about it. But darn it, he had tried to talk to Dennison a couple of times. Once he had asked him how he liked it here at Northern. Dennison had given him a long look that time before he said, "Well, I liked it better where I was last year."

What kind of an answer was that for a guy who wanted to make friends? To Billy, anybody who didn't like Northern was nuts. Why, there couldn't be a better school. He couldn't even *imagine* a better school than Northern.

Still, he thought about it. Dad sometimes asked casually about Dennison and if he was making any friends or what? So did Mother. If the coach and his parents thought he wasn't doing his job as captain, he'd try again to make Dennison part of the team, off the ice as well as on.

There'd be a chance after the next game. At the halfway point in the season, there was always a team party. They just had coffee, soft drinks and doughnuts after the game, with parents, a few teachers, and the coach attending. They usually held it in the cafeteria and the coach made a speech. That would be a good time to talk to Dennison. He'd try, he really would.

Northern's fifth game was to be against Grinstead. After the big opener with Jefferson Park, they had beaten Westmount Heights 6-3, Victoria 3-2, and Highgate 4-1. Grinstead also had a perfect four-win record. The luck of the scheduling was bringing the two top teams together.

Grinstead was tough. As play went from end to end the first two periods, Billy thought it was the closest game he'd ever been in. The Grinstead defensemen played it clean, but body-checked hard. One of their players, Jack Hayes, was a player of Billy's own type, go-go-go. Now Hayes was checking Dennison and doing a better job of it than anybody else had so far this season.

Coach Casey Gordon paced up and down behind his bench. The rink was full and partisan, and the mighty cheers for one of Billy's big stints on the ice were matched by applause for Jack Hayes.

S. S. PETER & PAUL SCHOOL
RICHMOND, MINNESOTA

As time went on, the crowd began to jeer Dennison almost as much as they cheered Hayes. "Hey Dennison, he's on you like glue," they'd yell. "How do you like carrying that guy in your back pocket all night, Dennison?"

In the third period there was still no score. The minutes flew by. Five minutes left. Four. Then two. In the last minute Grinstead came very close. The crowd cheered as Hayes made a particularly good play to bump Dennison off the puck in his own end and get a shot on goal. With the last 30 seconds ticking away, the crowd was still cheering that play. Then Dennison recovered the puck and started up the ice with his smooth, effortless stride.

His wingers were struggling to catch up. Hayes was skating backward in front of Dennison, watching closely, his stick out one way and his arm out the other way. Near the blue line, Dennison cut to his right toward the boards. Hayes stayed in front of him. Then Dennison moved over closer to the boards. He put on a burst of speed, as if to run the opening between

24

Hayes and the boards before Hayes could close the gap. It was a tight play and the crowd watched closely.

With Dennison's speed, Hayes suddenly saw that he couldn't cut him off while skating backward. He turned to skate forward and lunged to prevent Dennison from going through. At the last second Dennison slowed suddenly and shifted to the left, behind Hayes. Hayes tried to turn again, too. But he was moving too fast. Suddenly, his feet tangled and he pitched headlong into the boards with a loud crash.

The crowd gasped and jumped up, but Norm was concentrating on his game. He had already moved past the sprawled Hayes and he put a dazzling shift on the defenseman. Then he was going in with only the goalie to beat. Coolly, he faked a shot to the near corner. When the goalie moved to block it, Dennison changed the puck to his backhand, carried it across the goal, and tucked it into the other corner.

Goal. 1-0 for Northern, in the last second of play. The red light came on just before the blue one to end the game. But Hayes was still flat on the ice and writhing with pain.

Half the crowd hadn't been able to see the play well because it was close to the boards. All they had seen was the tangle of two bodies and sticks. Then Dennison was through and Hayes was down. A few people booed.

It still might not have been bad. Dennison was among the first back to Hayes' side. He was about to kneel beside him when one of the Grinstead players crosschecked him roughly out of the way. He made it look like Dennison had committed a foul against Hayes, and the Grinstead players didn't want him around now. The boos got louder. And Dennison, who had just scored one of the prettiest goals that Billy had ever seen, skated slowly to the bench with the boos of the crowd echoing in his ears.

In the excitement Billy hardly heard the boos. He had seen the play clearly, knew that Hayes had crashed himself into the boards. But in the general confusion nobody congratulated Dennison except Coach Gordon. The game was over, but the Northern players stayed on the ice to watch as a doctor hurried out of the stands, examined Hayes, and reported that his collar bone seemed to be broken.

After they had taken Hayes away on a stretcher the Northern players finally straggled to their dressing room, happy with the win, but subdued by the injury to Hayes.

When they got there, Dennison's equipment was piled neatly at his place on the bench. Dennison was gone.

He didn't turn up at the team party in the gymnasium. That really made Billy mad. This had been the night when he was going to make friends and try to start doing what Coach and his parents thought he really should have been doing all along. Darn the guy, anyway! How stuck-up and stand-offish could one guy be? This time he was going to find out why, for sure.

The next morning Billy went to the Dennison house and rang the bell. After a few minutes Mrs. Dennison came to the door. Billy had seen her at the Northern hockey games.

She spoke before Billy could say more than hello. Her voice was not kind at all. "Well, I must say I'm surprised to see you here."

"I just thought I'd . . . ah . . . like to have a talk with Norm," Billy said, a little nervously.

"He's gone downtown with his father," she said. "They're trying to get tickets to go to the city and see the pro game tonight. It was our way of showing him that we appreciated the goal he scored last night, even if none of you other precious people in Maple City did."

"But," Billy stammered, "we appreciated it! It was a great goal!" He'd forgotten all about what he'd come for, now. Norm's missing the party was gone entirely from his head. Now he could only think about what Norm's mother was saying and how Norm must feel.

"That's why the crowd booed him, was it?" she said coldly. "And that's why none of you on the team even went to him after he'd scored?"

"But Jack Hayes was hurt, and we . . . we . . . stayed out there," Billy said lamely.

She didn't say anything for a minute, gazing at him as if trying to make up her mind about something.

"Gee," Billy said, "I'm sorry if Norm thought . . . that we had . . . I mean, that we thought . . . ."

She looked at him again and said in a more friendly tone, "You'd better come in."

It was a small house, smaller than Billy's. Funny, he had thought Norm's family was well-off. The furniture was neat but worn. A set of shelves in the corner held a variety of trophies, and framed pictures of Norm in action were on the wall.

She had been sitting in a chair reading a newspaper. A coffee cup was on the table. She filled it in the kitchen and came back.

"You don't know much about Norm, do you?" she asked.

Billy shook his head. "Except that he scored his first goal in a regular game when he was only five years old," he said. "Most of the stories tell all about that. And about the rink that his Dad made for him in the side yard when you lived up north, so he could practice. And all the goals he has scored..."

"For the first time in his life," Mrs. Dennison said, "Norm's been lonely. Back home, sometimes, he was resented. I mean, when somebody gets to be that good, even a young boy like him, there are people who go to games just hoping to see his team get beaten.

"Before this it didn't matter so much because Norm had his own gang, his teammates, to back him up. He knew they were for him and it made everything else all right. But here..."

For the first time Billy thought of how he would feel if he had to move away from Northern and all his friends. And he remembered what Dad had said, weeks ago, about Norm needing to feel he was part of the team.

"Here," she continued, "he got the boos as usual, but none of the support. No one ever came to the house except some kids he walked home with, but they're more interested in books than sports."

"Well," Billy said, "I'm here now. I wanted to ask why he and you and his Dad didn't come to the team party last night, but I guess now I know." He searched for the right words.

"But honestly, I didn't know before. I mean, when somebody is as good as Norm is, you just don't think that anything bothers him, or that he needs friends, or...or..."

Just then a car pulled up outside and soon there were steps on the porch. The door opened and Norm's Dad came in, a balding, youngish-looking man whom Billy had seen at the games. Behind him was Norm, grinning and waving two tickets to the pro game. The grin suddenly disappeared when he saw Billy.

"Somebody here to see you, Norman," his mother said brightly.

Billy got up. He didn't know quite what to do, but all at once he felt that whatever it was, it shouldn't be soupy.

"Norm," he said, "in the confusion last night I didn't get to you to, ah, rumple your hair and whack the seat of your pants. I forgot to pile all over you for scoring that beautiful goal.

"The number of goals you score," Billy went on, starting to grin a little, "you see, we just decided that if we hammered you every time you scored a goal, you might be a hopeless cripple by the middle of the season. Then we'd be back to being a lousy team like we were before you came to Northern."

33

The jokes were coming easily now, the first in a long time, but they couldn't last forever. So Billy quit joking. He stuck out his hand.

"I'm sorry," he said. "We all should have been over here two months ago to welcome you."

He saw the smile begin to spread on Norm's face. It looked to Billy as if the battle was over. The load he had been carrying on his shoulders, he knew now, had started as jealousy and had gone on from there. He would know from now on to avoid that. Jealousy had made for a very heavy load.

"Ah, forget it," Norm said. "Who do we play next week, Jefferson Park again?"

"Jefferson Park. We're expecting four goals from you, just like the last time."

"Make it three," Norm said. "I can't count on those lucky deflections, like the first goal was."

"Lucky!" scoffed Billy. "That's skill, man, pure skill!"